1 Sundae

Example

To parents

Please remove the first sheet of stickers and give it to your child. This sheet is for exercises 1, 2 and 5. Up until exercise 3, your child will freely paste stickers onto a background. Encourage your child to peel the stickers off slowly and carefully so that the stickers do not tear. When he or she is finished, offer lots of praise and say "sundae" aloud while pointing to the word.

Paste the stickers as you like.

sundae

2 Birthday Cake

Example

To parents

The purpose of this exercise is for your child to learn how to peel off and paste stickers. This is not an easy skill for small children as it requires the ability to control intricate finger movements. When your child is finished, offer lots of praise.

Paste the stickers as you like.

birthday cake

How to use this book 1

Relax and enjoy!

Kumon's First Steps Workbooks are designed so that children and parents can learn and have fun together. Children learn best from active and participatory parents, so please help your child with the activities in this book. By helping, you are encouraging your child to develop a desire to learn, as well as laying the foundation for him or her to become a self-motivated learner.

How to choose glue and how to paste

If your child will be using glue for the first time, carefully select a type of glue that he or she will enjoy using.

Please choose a child-safe product in an easy-to-use container. Your child can use a glue stick but it is best for children to use glue that can be applied by hand. Children enjoy the tactile experience of spreading glue with their fingers.

▲ Please choose child-safe glue.

Tips for pasting

Line your table with scrap paper before your child starts. Have your child apply an appropriate amount of glue onto the tip of his or her middle finger and then spread it thinly on the part to be pasted. Please put the glue on the side with the glue symbol. When your child is applying glue, encourage him or her to hold the part with one hand and apply the glue onto it with the other. This is difficult for young children, so you can hold the paper for your child at first.

▲ Begin by placing glue onto the part. Then ask your child to use his or her finger to spread the glue on the designated area.

How to use this book 2

How to paste

Your child may already be familiar with playing with stickers, but perhaps he or she is used to just pasting them randomly. It may be difficult at first for your child to paste stickers onto a specific place, but be patient. In time, your child will master this skill.

It does not matter if your child cannot paste accurately or if the image he or she has created is not perfect. He or she will gradually learn to paste parts onto designated areas.

When your child is first attempting to paste a part onto a background, encourage him or her to place the edges down first and then slowly press the rest of the part into place. Your child will gradually learn how to align the parts correctly.

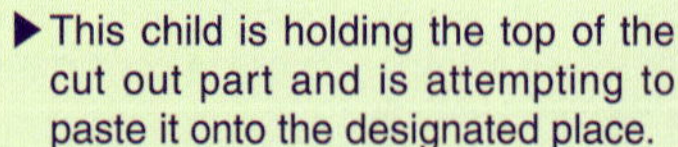

▶ This child is holding the top of the cut out part and is attempting to paste it onto the designated place.

3 Barbecue

Example

To parents
Please remove the second sheet of stickers and give it to your child. This sheet is to be used with exercises 3, 4, 6, 7 and 8. On this page, your child will practice pasting stickers wherever he or she would like. When your child has completed the activity, say "barbecue" aloud while pointing to the word.

Paste the stickers as you like.

barbecue

4 Juice

Done!

To parents
In the next series of exercises, your child will paste a sticker that corresponds to the shape of the white area on the page. Since the sticker for this page is round, your child will not have to worry about the sticker's orientation when placing it on the white area.

Paste the sticker onto the juice.

juice

5 Cheese

Done!

To parents
On this page, your child will paste a triangular sticker. Your child should pay close attention to the orientation of the sticker because this triangle has unequal sides. When your child is finished with the activity, say "cheese" aloud while pointing to the word.

Paste the sticker onto the cheese.

cheese

6 Red Pepper

Done!

To parents

You can encourage your child to pick the appropriate sticker from the sheet by saying something like, "Which sticker is for the red pepper?" When he or she has completed the exercise, offer praise and say "red pepper" aloud while pointing to the words.

Paste the sticker onto the red pepper.

red pepper

7 Chocolate

Done!

To parents

In this exercise, the sticker is a rectangle. Your child will practice aligning the edge of the sticker with the white space. Gradually guide your child to paste more precisely so that the sticker completely covers the white area. Still, it's not necessary to draw attention to a mistake, or to have him or her replace the sticker.

Paste the sticker onto the chocolate.

chocolate

8 Corn

To parents
This is the last activity in which your child will use stickers. On this page, the orientation of the sticker is important. Nonetheless, don't be concerned if your child places the sticker slightly off the white area.

Done!

Paste the sticker onto the corn.

corn

9 Fig

To parents

From this page on, your child will practice pasting with glue. In the beginning, you can put glue on the back of the cut out part for your child. These figs have a pattern, but do not be concerned if the cut out piece is not placed perfectly onto the picture. The most important thing is that your child enjoys pasting with glue. When your child has completed the exercise, say "fig" aloud while pointing to the word.

Paste the cut out part onto the fig.

fig

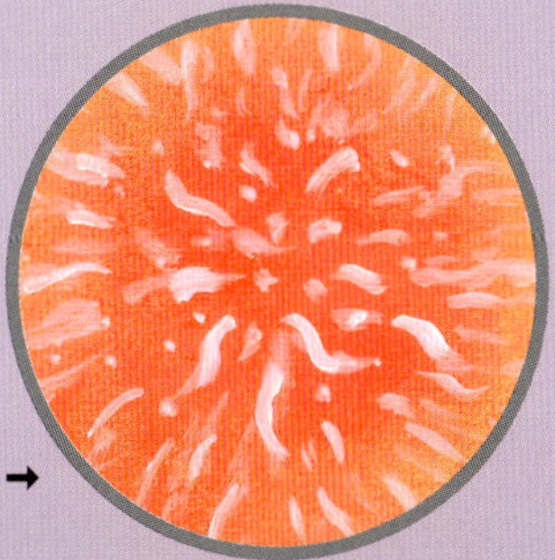

Parents: Please cut this part out for your child. →

10 Kiwifruit

Done!

To parents
If your child is having difficulty knowing where to place the part, point out the color of the kiwifruit as a hint. Don't be concerned if the image your child has created is not perfect.

Paste the cut out part onto the kiwifruit. kiwifruit

Parents: Please cut this part out for your child.

11

Avocado

Done!

To parents
Your child will paste a circular part on this page. When your child has completed the exercise, say "avocado" aloud while pointing to the word.

Paste the cut out part onto the avocado.

avocado

Parents: Please cut this part out for your child. →

Done!

12 Peach

To parents
Please do not be concerned if the image your child has created is not perfect. When he or she has completed the exercise, offer lots of praise.

Paste the cut out part onto the peach.

peach

13 Watermelon

To parents
This watermelon has seeds in it, but don't be concerned if the cut out piece is not placed perfectly onto the picture. It's not necessary to draw attention to a mistake or have your child try again.

Paste the cut out part onto the watermelon.

watermelon

Parents: Please cut this part out for your child. ➡

14 Tomato

To parents
It may be difficult for your child to place the cut out part onto this picture correctly. Offer lots of praise when your child has successfully chosen the right placement for the part.

Paste the cut out part onto the tomato.

tomato

Parents: Please cut this part out for your child. ↑

15 Celery

Done!

To parents
The white area is designed to be smaller than the cut out part so that no white will show if your child cannot paste neatly. If your child has difficulty pasting parts in the correct orientation, you can turn the part around when you hand it to him or her.

Paste the cut out part onto the celery.

celery

Parents: Please cut this part out for your child. ↑

16 Pickle Jar

Done!

To parents
The pattern and colors in this illustration should help your child figure out where to paste the cut out part. Don't be concerned if the image your child has created is not perfect.

Paste the cut out part onto the pickle jar.

pickle jar

Parents: Please cut this part out for your child. ↑

17 Pea Pod

Done!

To parents
It may be difficult for your child to place the cut out part onto this picture correctly. Offer lots of praise when your child has successfully chosen the right placement.

Paste the cut out part onto the pea pod.

pea pod

Parents: Please cut this part out for your child. ↑

18 Lollipop

To parents
The white area is designed to be smaller than the cut out part so that no white will show when your child pastes the part on top of it.

Paste the cut out part onto the lollipop.

lollipop

Parents: Please cut this part out for your child. ↑

19 Jello

To parents
Offer lots of praise when your child has successfully chosen the correct placement for the cut out part. Say "jello" aloud while pointing to the word.

Done!

Paste the cut out part onto the jello.

jello

Parents: Please cut this part out for your child. ↑

20 Breakfast

To parents
In this exercise, your child can paste the cut out parts onto the illustration wherever he or she pleases. It's okay not to follow the example on the right.

Example

Paste the yolk and bacon onto the plate.

breakfast

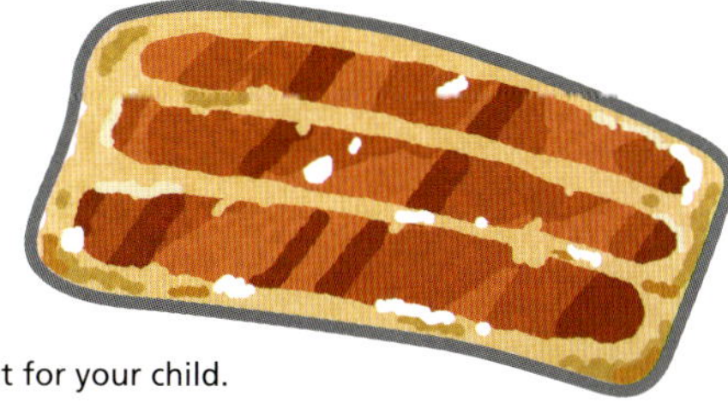

✂ Parents: Please cut these parts out for your child.

21 Steak

Example

To parents
Don't be concerned if the image your child has created is not perfect. When he or she has finished the activity, say something like,"This steak looks good!"

Paste the steak and carrots onto the plate.

steak

Parents: Please cut these parts out for your child.

22 Cupcake

To parents
Your child does not need to follow the example on the right. Encourage your child to use his or her own creativity.

Example

Paste the toppings onto the cupcakes.

cupcake

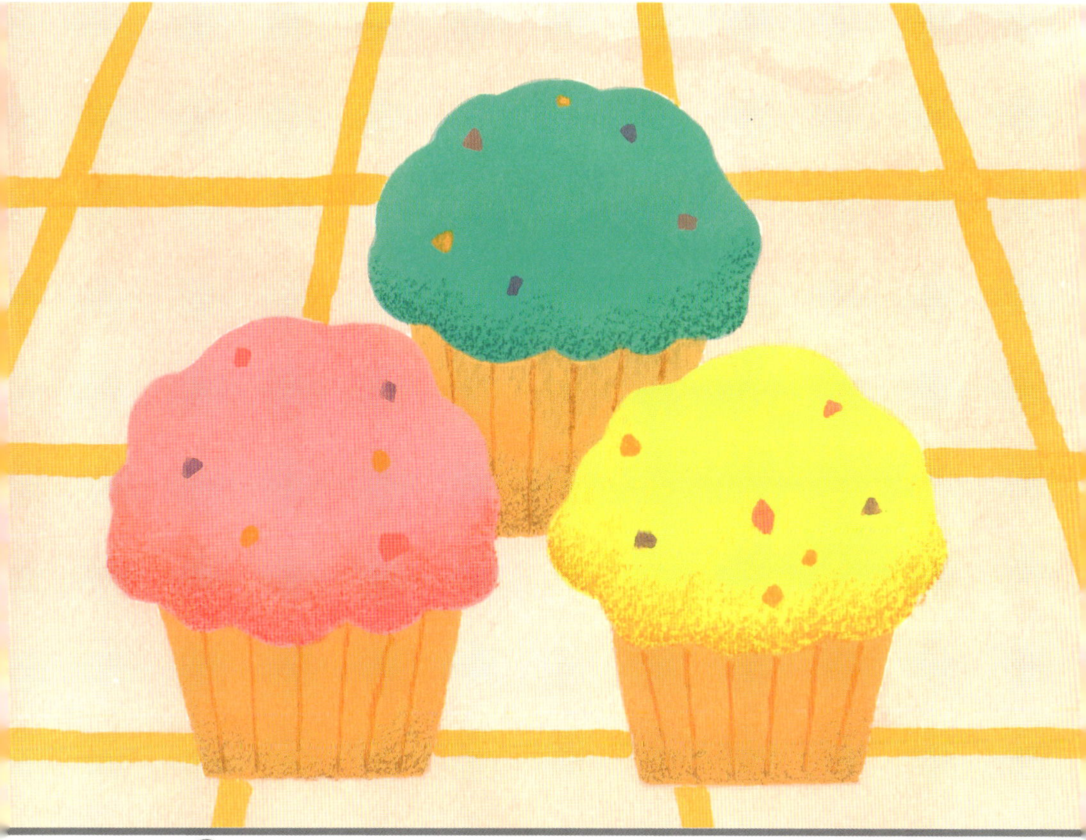

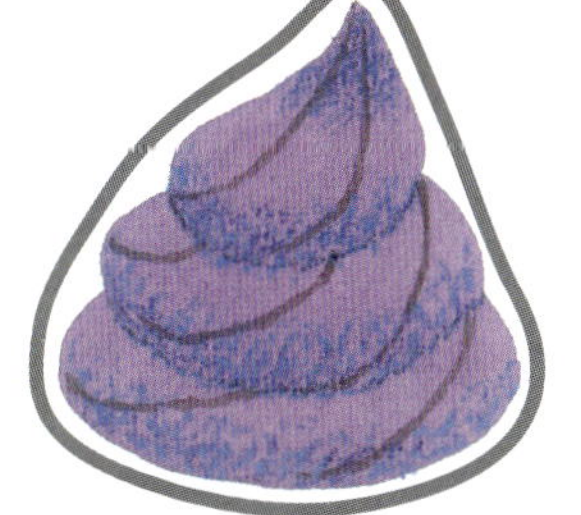

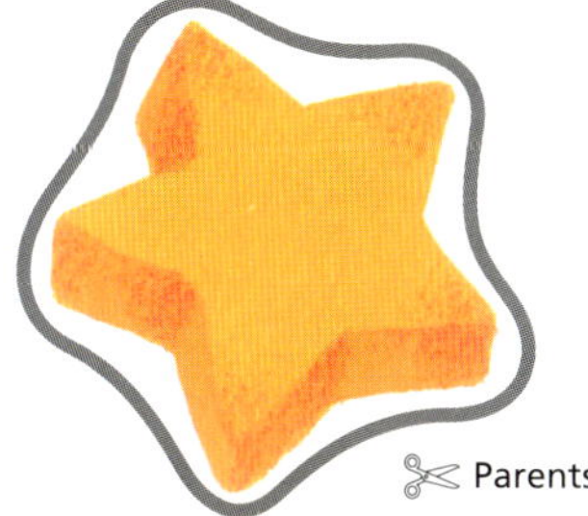

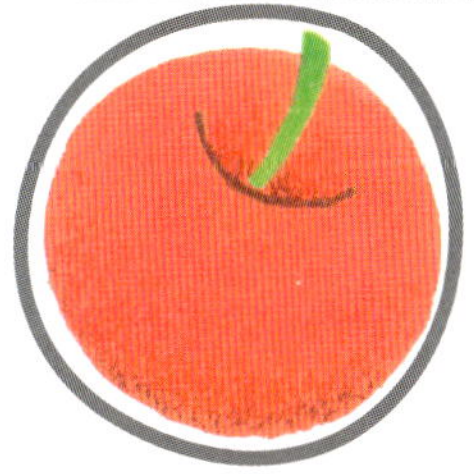

Parents: Please cut these parts out for your child.

23 Cookies

To parents

It may be a good idea to talk about the last time your child saw cookies on his or her dish. When he or she has completed the exercise, offer lots of praise.

Paste the cookies onto the dishes.

cookies

Parents: Please cut these parts out for your child.

24 Stew

Example

To parents
Your child can paste the cut out parts onto the illustration wherever he or she pleases. Encourage your child to be creative.

Paste the vegetables onto the pot.

stew

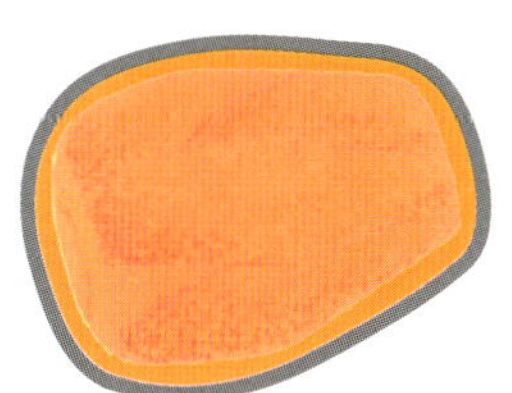
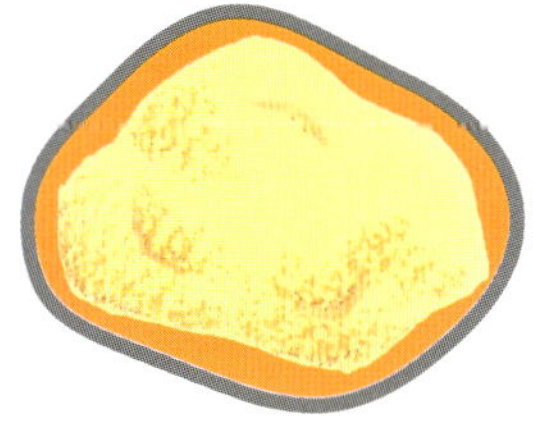
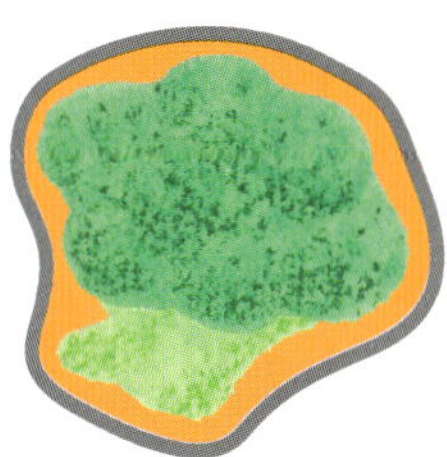

Parents: Please cut these parts out for your child.

25 Crab Cake

Example

To parents
Don't be concerned if the image your child has created is not perfect. When he or she has finished the activity, say something like, "These crab cakes look good!"

Paste the food onto the plate.

crab cake

Parents: Please cut these parts out for your child.

26 Picnic Basket

Example

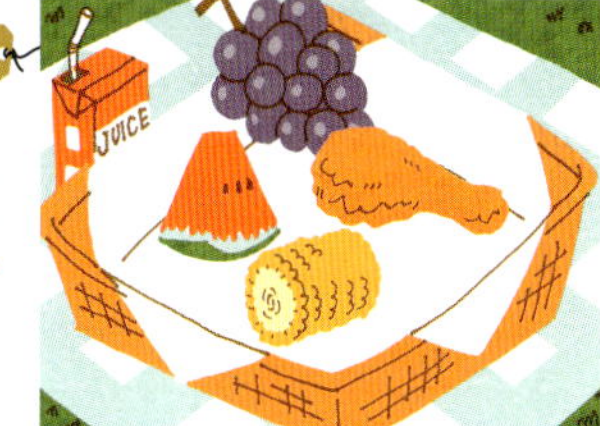

To parents
When he or she is finished, offer lots of praise and say something like, "Well done! It looks good," or "Let's go to the park with the picnic basket!"

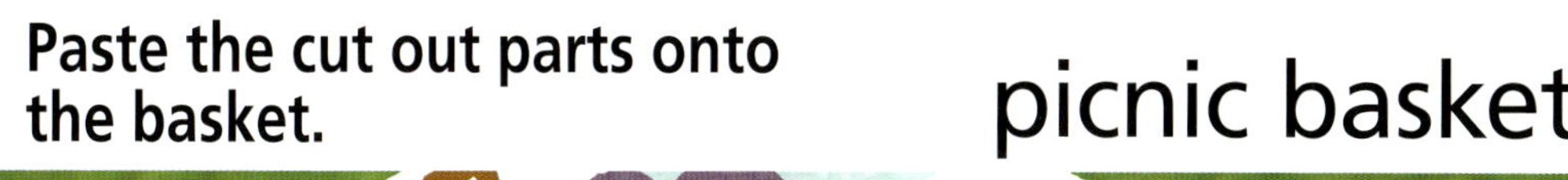

Paste the cut out parts onto the basket.

picnic basket

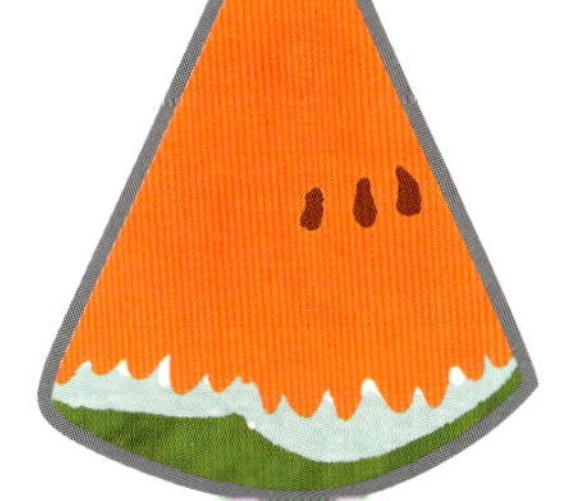

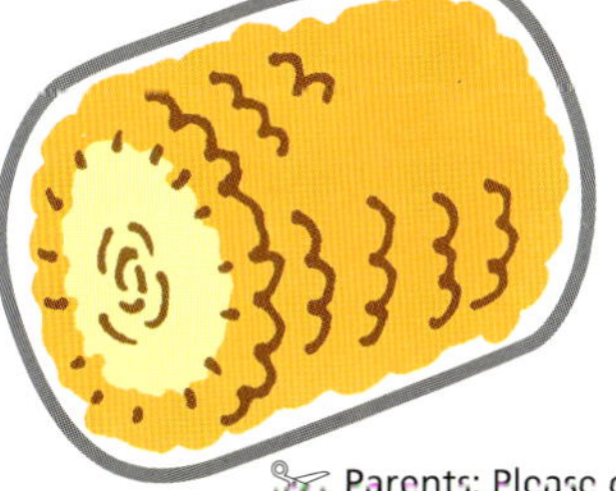

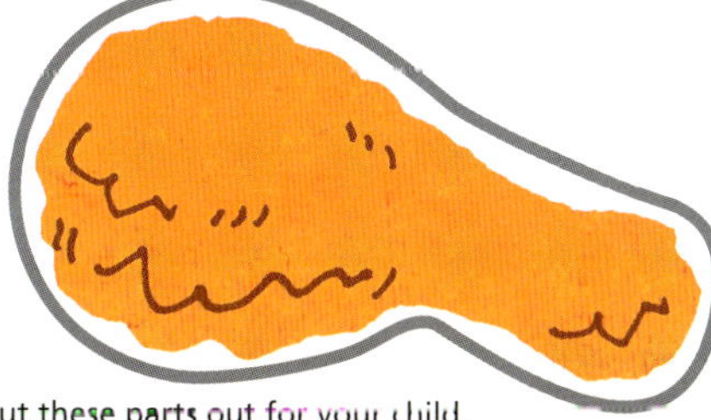

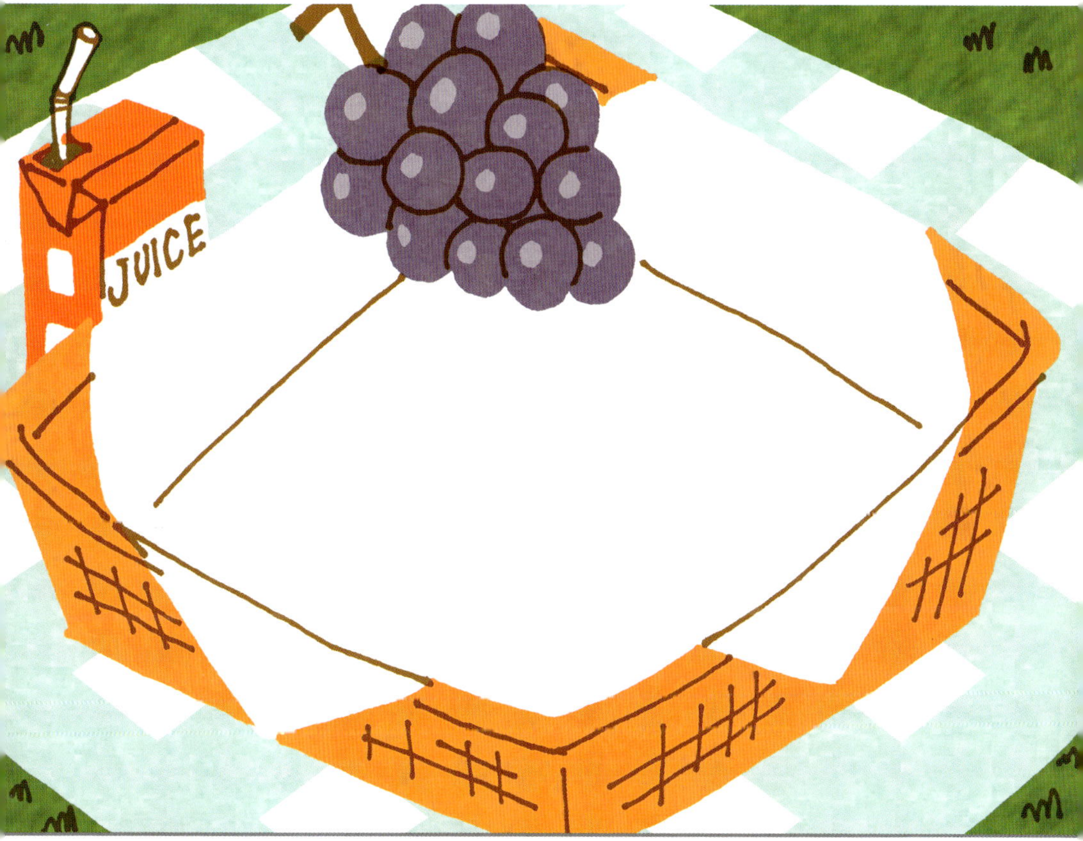

Parents: Please cut these parts out for your child.

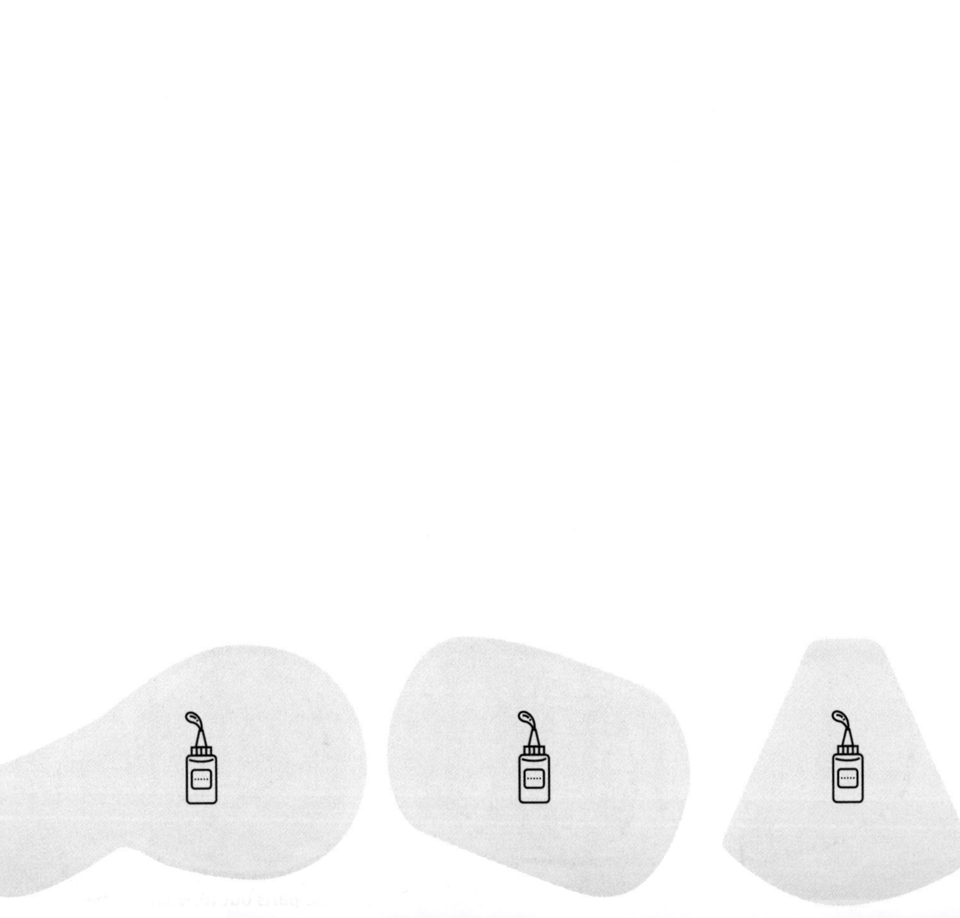

27 Lunch Box

To parents

Pasting small parts is not easy for young children. When your child has completed the exercise, offer lots of praise, and say something like, "Well done!" or "What's in the box?"

Paste the cut out parts onto the lunch box.

lunch box

Parents: Please cut these parts out for your child.

28 Cereal

Example

To parents
Your child does not need to copy the example on the right. When he or she is finished, offer lots of praise and say something like, "It looks good!" or "What did you have for breakfast today?"

Paste the cut out parts onto the cereal.

cereal

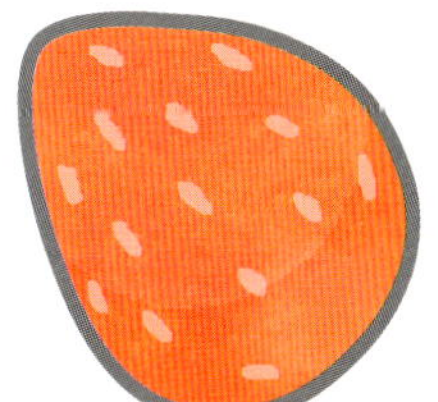
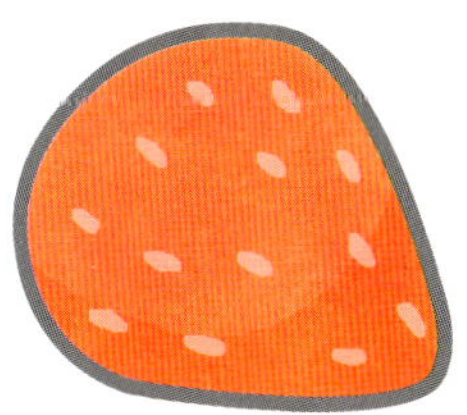

Parents: Please cut these parts out for your child.

29 Sushi

Example

To parents
Your child can paste the cut out parts on whichever mound of rice he or she pleases. Encourage your child to be creative.

Paste the cut out parts onto the rice.

sushi

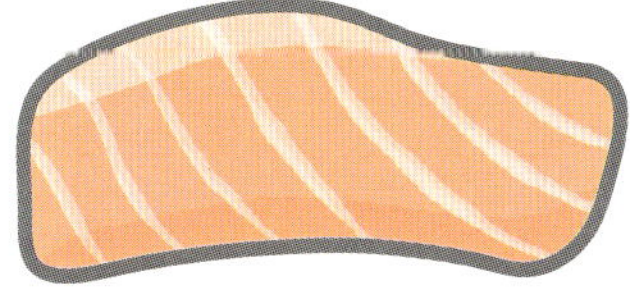

Parents: Please cut these parts out for your child.

30 Carrot

To parents

Have your child look at the sample on the right before starting to paste. Show your child how to fit the pieces together correctly if he or she seems to be having difficulty. Your child doesn't need to apply glue all along the edge—just a few dabs will be fine.

Paste the cut out parts onto the white area to complete the carrot.

carrot

Parents: Please cut along ——— for your child.

31 Pineapple

To parents
Encourage your child to try to arrange the parts of the pineapple correctly without your help.

Paste the cut out parts onto the white area to complete the pineapple.

pineapple

Parents: Please cut along ▬▬▬ for your child.

32 Eggplant

To parents
Before using glue, tell your child to place the cut out parts onto the white area to see which way they should go.

Paste the cut out parts onto the white area to complete the eggplant.

eggplant

Parents: Please cut along ▬▬▬ for your child.

33 Ice Cream

To parents
Encourage your child to place the parts several different ways before pasting them with glue. When he or she is finished, offer lots of praise and say something like, "Well done! It looks good."

Paste the cut out parts onto the white area to complete the ice cream cone.

Parents: Please cut along ▬▬▬ for your child.

ice cream

34 Salad

To parents
It's okay if your child has pasted a part with the wrong orientation or in the wrong place. It's more important that your child enjoys pasting.

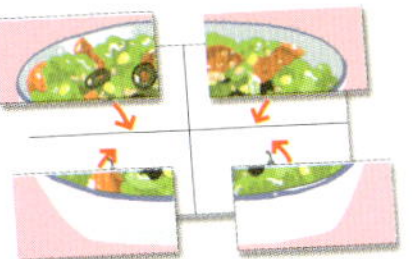

Paste the cut out parts onto the white area to complete the salad.

salad

✂ Parents: Please cut along ▬▬▬ for your child.

35 Hamburger

To parents
Encourage your child to arrange the cut out parts correctly without your help. Offer help only if it is needed.

Paste the cut out parts onto the white area to complete the hamburger.

hamburger

Parents: Please cut along ——— for your child.

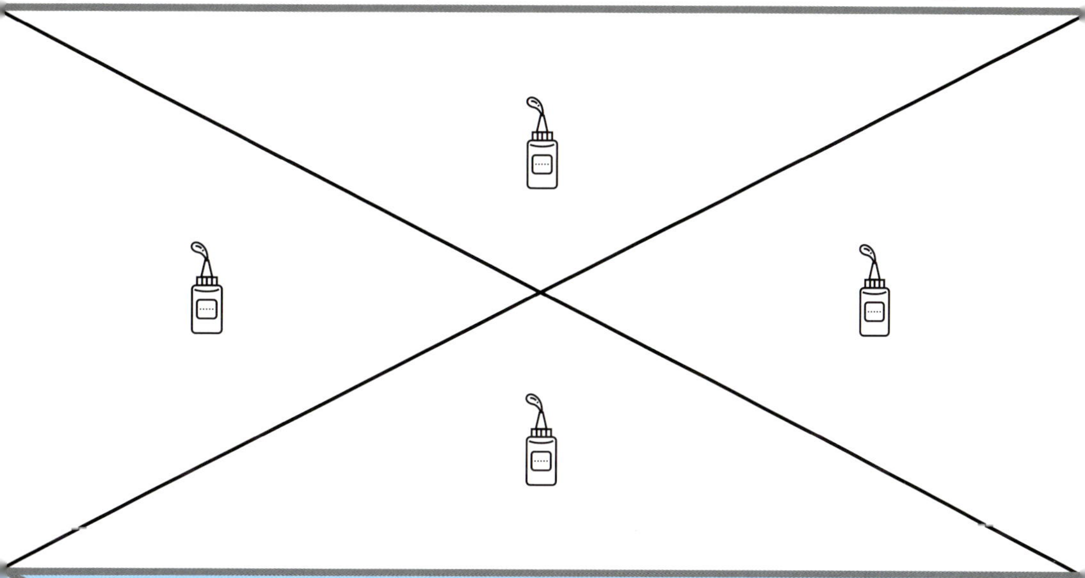

36 Tea Sandwiches

To parents
From this page forward, your child will arrange and paste 6 pieces of an illustration. Don't be concerned if the image your child has created is not perfect.

Paste the cut out parts onto the white area to complete the tea sandwiches.

Parents: Please cut along ▬▬▬ for your child.

tea sandwiches

37 Waffle

Done!

To parents

It may be a good idea to place the cut out parts onto the illustration to check their placement before using glue. Encourage your child to try and figure out how to create the picture from the 6 pieces.

Paste the cut out parts onto the white area to complete the waffle.

waffle

Parents: Please cut along ▬▬▬ for your child.

38 Curry and Rice

To parents
If your child seems to be having difficulty, offer to help. When your child has finished, offer lots of praise.

Paste the cut out parts onto the white area to complete the curry and rice.

curry and rice

Parents: Please cut along ▬▬▬ for your child.

39 Sub

To parents

This is the last exercise in this workbook. Compare your child's work on this exercise with his or her earlier work. You will probably notice a lot of progress in your child's ability to arrange and paste parts correctly. Offer lots of praise for his or her accomplishment!

Paste the cut out parts onto the white area to complete the sub.

sub

Parents: Please cut along ▬▬ for your child.

KUMON

Certificate of Achievement

____

is hereby congratulated on completing

Let's Sticker & Paste! Food Fun

Presented on ______________________________, 20______

____

Parent or Guardian